One Before Bedtime

One Before Bedtime

Tales of mystery, fantasy and suspense

Nathaniel S. Johnson

atmosphere press

© 2023 Nathaniel S. Johnson

Published by Atmosphere Press

Cover design by Ronaldo Alves

No part of this book may be reproduced without permission from the author except in brief quotations and in reviews. This is a work of fiction, and any resemblance to real places, persons, or events is entirely coincidental.

Atmospherepress.com

Contents

Bullyboys............................3

Child's Play..........................7

A Party of Eight.....................17

Early Checkout......................25

Her SweetBerry.....................35

You Can Bank on It..................47

Night Riders........................51

Old Thompson......................55

Beasley's Machines..................59

Dr. Hodgkins Goes to Heaven..........63

Bullyboys

At school, Caleb suffered the bullyboys because he would not join in and play ball. His parents said, "Ignore them; they will stop." His teachers' answer never changed: "Bully them back." After school, Caleb found a secret route out and then disappeared.

"Where does he go?" asked Billy, the gigantic bully.

"To the woods," mumbled Bobby, the dullest bully.

"To talk with the *animals*," giggled Ben, the smallest bully.

Caleb had secrets. He would go to the woods to meet his faithful friends: the wolves and the black bears, the coyotes and cougars—all were his allies, but none offered solutions for the meanness of man.

One day, the bullyboys ganged up to lay down their rules. They grabbed Caleb and made their demand: Be at the ball field Saturday night or beware.

"Why should I?" cried Caleb.

"Because you haven't played ball." Billy furled his shirtsleeves to show his muscles.

"Because you're a dweeb," mocked Bobby.

"Because your clothes are so weird, and so is your hair," muttered Ben.

"Be there, or be dead!" Billy growled, giving Caleb a shove. The bullyboys snickered and went on their way.

On Saturday evening, Caleb answered the summons and came to the ball field where the bullyboys were gathered, grinning, and waving their bats. It was early in June, on the night of a full moon, and though Caleb was frightened, he stood fast.

"We thought you'd wimp out," said Billy, flexing his chest.

"I'm not afraid."

"You *must* be," said Bobby, caressing his bat.

"You *will* be," Ben said with a glower.

"I *won't* be," said Caleb, returning their glare.

"Now, step to the plate," said Billy, forcing Caleb to bat. "Stand tall and play ball." Billy strode to the mound. Caleb walked to the plate and shouldered his bat, but before he could blink, a ball buzzed by, nearly hitting his head.

"Stee-RIKE!" gloated Billy with glee.

"I wasn't ready," Caleb said. Without warning, a second ball screamed past, narrowly missing his knees.

"Stee-rike-TWO!" bellowed Billy.

"Not even close," cried Caleb.

"I'll show you what's *close*," raged Billy as a third ball flew straight into Caleb's belly. Grabbing his stomach, Caleb keeled over, gasping in pain.

All went silent. The moon rose, and groans broke the air, growing to yowls heard all over town. Unholy mewling came from all sides, and when the bullies saw them, they went pale. Out of the twilight, limping shadows loped onto the field, their mouths pink and wet, their eyes glowing coals. The rumbling grew fiercer until Caleb yelled, "Silence." The bullies stared at Caleb, standing fearless and proud.

"Tell them to go," demanded Billy, trembling.

"They want you for dinner," said Caleb, unsmiling.

"We never meant harm," said Bobby, weeping.

"You have not spoken," said Caleb, pointing at Ben. "Give us your answer before they get hungry." The animals circled, watching the bullies with eyes smoking; their choler was rising.

"I'm sorry," said Ben, shaking in shame, his trousers gone wet.

Soon, a convoy rode out from town; villagers heard the

strange sounds, but they saw only bullies cringing and sullen when they arrived. They laughed at the one with soaked pants, another quivering, white as chalk, a third kneeling—his hands clasped in prayer. When told the tale of fierce creatures, folks reckoned the bullies were drunk, turned away, and drove off.

Caleb never came back, nor did his congress of friends. His parents said he had gone traveling; his teachers dismissed him—no more trouble at school. Yet, the village remembered, for once every year, on a warm night early in June, they hear animals calling and, high overhead, a young boy's laughter. They search but see only the moon.

Child's Play

- Dedicated to the memory of Ray Bradbury -

Blooming June. Morrisville rejoices in summer's flowers: Schools closing, family picnics in the park, canoeing on the Nashoba River, swimming at Blake's Pond, gathering blueberries in the south woods, and, in a month, the much-anticipated Morrisville 4th of July festivities. This week, besides vacations, shorts and short-sleeves, boating and bathing suits, beach balls, and barbeques, something extraordinary has this town stirred up.

Villagers have been gossiping and texting about *him* all week—that odd man who came to town last Sunday morning in a loudly-painted gypsy van, drove straight up Main Street, and then moved in and took ownership of Ben's Village Antiques. Old Ben died a year ago; his shop had remained shut and shuttered—until today. Who *is* Silas Keebler, that lanky, pale man with black, slicked-back hair, enormous, peering brown eyes, and old-fashioned attire? Who is he, and why has he come to Morrisville?

Three women chattered over coffee and muffins in Popovers after their morning jog. "Been over to Ben's since the new owner moved in?" Heavily into her forties and forever inquisitive, Connie Brooks was madly curious. "Maybe we should take a peek."

Kim Anderson, early thirties, drummed her fingers on the table. "Creeps me out—that weird face staring through the shop window. I hear the whole place got infested with cobwebs."

Connie shivered.

Joan Finney, the youngest, suddenly leaned forward as if to reveal a secret. "Perhaps he's from outer space—come to spy before they land."

Connie set down her mug. "Before *who* lands?"

"The aliens, of course," Joan whispered.

Kim jumped. "What?"

Joan narrowed her eyes and pointed her finger upwards while simultaneously humming the theme from *The Twilight Zone*, and they all laughed.

★ ★ ★

Morrisville, New Hampshire—crouched right over the Massachusetts border—a green and agreeable village, home to young marrieds with kids and a growing group of reluctant retirees, each of whom is restless and longing for excitement: one last fling, one final journey.

Their summer days amble by, dozing at the library, swapping rumors over coffee at Popovers, congregating after church on weekends, or at family picnics in the park while swatting mosquitoes at the summer band concerts. All are awaiting the great event: the Morrisville Annual July 4th Patriots Day Grand Parade. There would be lobsters and watermelon at the bandstand, pony rides, fireworks, and a bonfire at sunset. Nobody, however, anticipated how peculiar this year's Fourth would be.

Popovers on Main Street, serving gourmet coffee and healthy muffins, was entirely staffed by young men and women in trendy vests and caps. Light classical music drifted out from overhead speakers, blending with the clink of silverware and muffled clatter of dishes in the kitchen. Sitting across from Connie and friends on this sunny morning, Doc Peterson and Ray Trumbull sparred with young Jimmy Walden, the druggist.

"Won't be long before the big parade." That was Doc Peterson: heals them, births them, buries them—done so for more than forty years. "Our kids always hung around at home in the sixties on the Fourth." Doc waggled his finger at Jimmy. "Today, they just run off and do whatever they want."

Jimmy shook a tousle of curly red hair. "The sixties? Come on, Doc! You're still talking stone-age stuff." Jimmy's freckled face grinned as if he were ten again.

"Noses in their phones all day—can't even think to say *hello*," grumbled the balding Ray Trumbull, proprietor of Trumbull's Lumber and Hardware. He'd inherited the business from his dad nearly two decades ago. "They get whatever they want, whenever they want it, not like in my day."

Jimmy snorted. "Ray, in *your* day, dinosaurs still roamed the earth."

"When *we* were kids, a car was a luxury few enjoyed, especially in high school," admonished Doc Peterson, gaunt and bearded. "Now, they've *all* got one!" Doc enjoyed ribbing Jimmy—the Jimmy he brought into this world.

Ray made a sour face. "You know, Doc, Jimmy was a good kid until he grew up." He gave Jimmy a soft nudge.

Jimmy yawned. "Ray, with any luck, I'll *never* grow up."

Doc looked around. "Met the new man at Ben's yesterday; seems nice enough." He leaned forward. "Weird looking, though; wears strange old clothes. Talks funny, too."

"Maybe that's why he's into antiques—he likes *old* things, like many funny *old* people around here." Jimmy grinned, stood up, patted Doc on the shoulder, saluted the kitchen staff, and promptly departed the coffee shop.

And thus, their lives slip onward, tranquil and uneventful; some fret and worry they might soon die—not of senility, but through sheer boredom.

★ ★ ★

On weekends and after school, up and down Main Street, at Rollins Park, and all over the village, Morrisville youth on bikes, scooters, or skateboards hurry past everyone with indifference, each submerged beneath their private cocoons of earbuds. Watching reproachfully from sidewalk benches, seniors squint at this vernal new world passing them by, a world that clutches its mobile media as if on life-support.

"Rude!" a gray woman barked at her wrinkled friend.

"When I was a girl, we always said 'Good morning, sir; good morning, ma'am,'" snapped the wrinkled one.

It's the last morning of classes across town at the high school. The excitement is barely containable as drama coach Harold Benson addresses a group of fidgety students in the auditorium, all mesmerized by the wall clock above his head.

"Now, before you run off, listen up! I've written a *new* play, and I'm looking for a good cast."

Muted applause issued forth, with all eyes still fixed on the clock.

"Young and old, all kinds of roles."

An eager student in jeans raised her hand. "What's it about, Mr. Benson?"

"It's about *you!*" he cried. "*All* of you . . . all of *us.*"

★ ★ ★

Harold Benson had been offered a retirement package but refused it. Instead, he volunteered to stay on as drama director and lead the Christmas pageant in the Morrisville Town Square once more, as he had done for more years than he could remember. Harold still had his senses and a semblance of his youth, but Jerold Manning, the school principal, had another opinion.

"It's a play about growing young, hope and laughter; never giving up...or giving in."

"We want you *back* next year, Mr. Benson!" someone shouted, and suddenly the bell clamored. Vibrant youth flooded the exit, joining the exodus to a rushing summer, one seemingly already in progress.

"Tell everyone about my play—it's about your town and our town. And everyone has a part!" Harold called out over the din. "Don't forget; there'll also be a prize—the best acting award."

"What's the prize?" called a young man, holding his cell phone and hanging halfway out the door.

"A special spot in the 4th of July Parade!" Harold replied, wagging his manuscript. "And you'll be on community TV. You'll be famous!"

That afternoon, on a vacant stage in the high-school auditorium, Harold Benson read his entire play to an empty house, speaking all the parts and listening to his voice resound within the dim and cavernous space. He strained for the sound of applause and, in the end, bowed to his invisible audience.

Unseen, in the darkened, far end of the hall with arms folded, Principal Manning grumbled, shook his head, and slipped away.

★ ★ ★

By week's end, the word had swelled and spilled over town, and on Saturday, a bold headline blared across the *Morrisville Daily Times*. "Remember Your Youth? Join The Fun!" Connie read the announcement aloud to her group at Popovers: "Harold Benson announced auditions at the high school and has invited everyone in Morrisville. There will be prizes for the best actors and actresses—even seniors, presenting themselves as if they were young once again."

"Seems like everyone wants a part," Kim yawned. "Well, you won't catch *me* showing up in some kiddy costume."

"Sounds like fun." Joan clapped her hands. "I'm going for it!"

Connie shook her head. "Principal Manning is looking to

get Harold out. It doesn't look good for him, even with this play."

"But the kids *love* him," Joan insisted, sipping her coffee.

Kim stood up to leave. "Well, Harold's sixty-five, isn't he? The town must cut the school budget next year anyway. When you gotta go, you gotta go."

Teenagers sitting on a bench outside Popovers were also reading about the play in the paper. Their take was slightly different:

"A stupid idea."

"What's the point?"

"Grown-ups should just grow up!"

"Yeah, old folks should act their age."

They all snickered.

★ ★ ★

Jimmy Walden desperately wanted a lead role in Harold Benson's play. That week, he led villagers rummaging through dusty trunks, buried boxes, and moldy suitcases in attics, closets, basements, and garages, urging them to search for clothing, toys, photos, and the treasures of childhood. However, none found fitting apparel nor the playthings they once cherished. When they grew discouraged, Jimmy piped up. "Hey! Let's try the antique shop; maybe Silas Keebler has what we want."

On the Saturday evening before their visit, someone saw Silas Keebler peering through the soap-covered picture window, and when a harvest moon rose, the window and the shop were spotless, and the oil lamps lit—as if Old Ben himself had returned.

The searchers, led by Piper Jimmy, proceeded to the antique shop on Sunday afternoon. At the same time, the new owner—all dapper and youthful—waited for them in the doorway, beckoning one and all into his emporium, now shiny and sparkling clean. Silas Keebler held up a wooden wand tipped with a gold star in one hand.

"Come in! Come in, everyone is welcome, and I have all you need. Everything is here. Everything is genuine, and, for today only, *everything* is on sale."

Connie and Jimmy looked at one another and smiled. Silas Keebler, meanwhile, leaped gamely about, seizing wooden toys resting on shelves, holding up children's books, teddy bears, and other soft animals, urging everyone to explore.

"Look!" Alice, the librarian, held up a little girl's pink and white party dress. "It's the same I had when I was nine.

Jeffrey, a retired police officer, clasped a red and black metal locomotive to his chest. "This was the train my dad gave me for Christmas."

Connie looked down at Silas Keebler's soft animal cradled in her arms and sobbed. "Eeyore, folks. It's *my* Eeyore."

Jimmy tapped Connie on the shoulder and pointed towards Ray Trumbull, standing in the doorway, looking like a lost little boy. Silas pulled an object from a trunk filled with vintage clothes and presented a child's railroad engineer's cap to Ray. He then turned and waved his wand. It breathed an ineffable stream of yellow stars that lit up the shop. Everyone gasped and smiled; some even shed happy tears.

Arms cradling memories, hearts filled with anticipation, The New Morrisville Players traveled back into time—back to the dreams of their childhood. But when darkness descended and everyone prepared to leave the shop, they were astonished to discover that all the price tags were blank and that Silas Keebler had disappeared.

★ ★ ★

On the last Sunday in June, Harold Benson welcomed a large and boisterous turnout at the high-school auditorium. Carrying the glorious remnants of their past, villagers arrived in costume, crowding the stage and flawlessly playing their roles. Harold's play was an outstanding success, and the whole town cheered. All seemed pleased except Principal Manning, who understood nothing and returned to his office to prepare Harold Benson's layoff notice.

★ ★ ★

July exploded, and suddenly the town's big day was at hand. Lawn and beach chairs and all other sitting conveniences were positioned en route. A marching band drummed down Main Street at two o'clock, followed by homemade floats and horse-drawn carts. An open car filled with the town's antique dignitaries, pursued by uniformed Scouts, Cubs, Brownies, firefighters, police officers, and war veterans, paraded before cheering, flag-waving villagers.

Then, something happened. Heads swiftly turned when a group of children trooped up the street bathed in a golden glow, all dressed in period apparel. Waving a wand tipped by a yellow star, they were led by a young boy with long hair and huge, peering brown eyes. When they drew closer, the crowd craned their heads to stare, then grew silent, astonished by what was coming.

Standing together on the sidewalk, stunned by the spectacle before them, Connie Brooks, Doc Peterson, and the village watched the children pass. A young boy with bright red hair walked alone, grinning.

Doc Peterson called out, "Jimmy? That you?" Connie waved at a young girl. "Joan?" The children, immersed in their glow, did not hear the calls. At the sight of Ray Trumbull, transformed into a young boy wearing his engineer's cap, Doc Peterson waved, burst into tears, and tried to call out.

"Doc! Doc!" Connie grabbed Doc's arm. "We must go see Keebler. Now!"

Doc Peterson tried to pull away. "No! I cannot go."

"Come on. We *must*." Connie held tight.

"No, Connie! It's too late." Connie tugged at Doc Peterson's arm, edging him away from the crowd. "Why do you make me go, Connie? Can't you see? I'm way too old."

Connie grew impatient. "You're *never* too old, and it's *never* too late. Now, come on!" Connie pulled Doc away from the parade and up the now-empty Main Street, the sound of the marching bands fading while they walked. Dusk descended, and a full moon rose on the horizon. "Hurry, Doc. Almost there."

When they stopped—only a few yards away from what was once Old Ben's Antique Shop—Connie's joyful face crumpled in anguish. Both stared at the hastily drawn, hand-lettered sign tacked to the door:

> Out of Business
> PROPERTY FOR SALE
> Anderson Realty

For time immemorial, Independence Day has arrived at countless Morrisvilles across America. Yet, it was an extraordinary Fourth in this town—for a few hopeful and very fortunate youngsters.

A Party of Eight

Mike and Mary Ann Generoso would help you with anything: a family crisis, a flat tire, a flooded basement, a lost dog, or just commiseration about the worsening economy. Their Old Orchard Inn, a classic New England Colonial, complete with ocean views from its hillside perch on Gull Cove, was a perennially popular B&B.

The Generoso's survival secret: keeping their property up, rates down, and plenty of Mike's freshly baked bread and muffins available every morning. Innkeeping was an arduous and full-time commitment, but, as Mary Ann often said, "We're in it for the long haul." The Old Orchard did reliable repeat business, but being up at five, in bed by nine, seven days a week, was not easy, especially in winter. The Generosos, now in their mid-fifties and sprouting gray hairs, often wished that the lottery, or a long-lost uncle, would offer an early retirement.

Amusing and charming, Mike and Mary Ann were well-liked by many in town. Occasionally they were entertained by friends in Boston with whom they would share an evening meal on Sunday, their one night off. While the Generosos were generous to family and friends, they could be frugal. When gasoline prices rose and the economy declined, they adjusted rates downward. If their parking lot was empty, so was the swimming pool.

Their other friends, Jim and Jody Winston—older, quiet, and reserved—operated a modest real estate office a mile outside Gull Cove. Once well-to-do, their commissions waned as housing prices fell, and although they never admitted to their plight, they still had some savings and pretended not to worry. The Winstons shared frequent meals at the Inn on weekends. Jim and Jody were always available whenever the Generosos offered dinner, especially if the venue was one of Boston's fancy restaurants.

The Generosos also regularly entertained Todd and Karen Jewell, a retired couple who lived in the village and were considered authentic Gull Cove eccentrics. Todd painted *ho-hum* seascapes in oils and watercolors that even tourists found unremarkable. Karen opened her card shop in spring and closed it for the winter. After Christmas, when the tourists left town, activity at Gull Cove slowed down.

The Generosos enjoyed the Jewells' company at dinner, with Todd telling risqué jokes and Karen doing wicked imitations of everyone in town. Thus, the Jewells were frequent dinner guests. Over time, Todd's paintings and Karen's cards filled the lobby and bedrooms of The Old Orchard Inn. Nobody in town could figure out how the Jewells ever made ends meet.

One evening Alan and Betsy Bonner, the Generoso's oldest friends and part-time financial advisors from Boston, telephoned to announce that Betsy was turning fifty. They were planning a big birthday bash at one of Back Bay's best restaurants, and it would be on a Sunday in June. Would the Generosos like to attend?

"Betsy, the Birthday Girl, ain't all that thrilled about fifty," Alan whispered to Mary Ann after Betsy got off the phone, "so I'm going to cheer her up with a big do at Jean Jacques. She enjoys the Winstons and adores Karen Jewell, so maybe we'll invite all of them."

"Great idea," Mary Ann replied, mentally calculating the tab. "Sure you can afford all this?" The Bonners had been pleading poverty for the past two years, and the bash at Jean Jacques would be big-ticket.

"We might ask guests to contribute drinks, champagne, or dessert. I don't know, Mary Ann. I haven't added it all up just yet." Alan paused, waiting for a reply.

Well, I have, thought Mary Ann, *and it's enormous.* "Sure, we'll help, Alan," she said. "Let's chat about it later, OK?"

"Oh man, you guys are so generous!" Alan burbled, sounding more relaxed and relieved. "Guess that's why we love our *Generosos*, isn't it?"

"Well, tell Betsy that fiftieth birthdays come only once in a lifetime, so she should just enjoy herself."

"Thanks, Mary Ann. Cheers!"

Mary Ann put down the phone. *Uh oh, better tell Mike.*

Mike groaned when he heard about Alan's proposal. "Don't mind chipping in for drinks, but I recall we once footed the whole bill for *my* birthday."

"Good thing we weren't at Jean Jacques!"

"And I hope the Winstons don't forget their credit cards again," Mike said.

"I don't think the Jewells even *use* credit cards anymore," Mary Ann replied.

"Maxed out, no doubt." Mike was not impressed by The Jewell's grasp of business affairs and took a dim view of their bohemian lifestyle.

"I feel a bit sorry for all these folks," Mary Ann said.

"Not *too* sorry, I hope. We've got no room in our bank balance for a moocher's banquet at one of Boston's best."

★ ★ ★

The party of eight gathered at Jean Jacques on the second Sunday in June. They were seated at a private banquet room overlooking Boston Harbor, with a singing waiter and twin coolers chilling Dom Perignon. Alan Bonner was late, as usual. His face and neck bore a tell-tale crimson when he finally arrived. The reason for his delay was evident.

"Ah, *there* you are," announced Betsy, at a high sound level, smacking her heavily painted lips. "We thought you'd died—"

"And gone to Heaven," Alan finished, looking around and grinning stupidly at his assembled guests. "Let's have some Champagne!" he bellowed, gripping the table and Betsy's chair before belching quietly.

After the maître d' made his obligatory appearance, wishing everyone *bon appétit* and following the customary birthday felicitations, the party of eight began chattering. *How well everyone looks, what a nice restaurant. Wasn't the weather lousy this spring? Are you going away for Christmas? Let's hope home heating oil prices don't skyrocket this winter; how much lower can the economy go?*

Time for more champagne. Just as their singing waiter entered the room to croon his suggestions from the chef, Mike's cell phone rang.

"Excuse me," Mike said, looking at his phone. "It's my son," and stood up to leave.

Mary Ann looked concerned. "Sorry, everyone, I better go too; it's probably Billy, looking for his dinner." They left the room together. When finally alone, Mike switched on the speakerphone.

"What is it, Billy?"

"Dad, Mom—get home right away. Now!" Billy was shouting.

"Billy, what's wrong?" Mary Ann asked, wondering if the Inn was going up in flames.

"Please, get home, but don't drive too fast. I have amazing news, but nobody must know. *Nobody*! Understand?"

Mike was irritated. "Look, Billy, this is a birthday party and—"

"Dad, you *must* believe this is too important. But it's a good thing, I guarantee. Really. Tell all your friends the toilets are leaking, but you must come home *immediately*."

Mike and Mary Ann stared at one another. Billy had never

behaved this way before.

"All right," Mike said, switching off his phone, "but if we get home and find Billy drunk again, there will be big trouble."

The Generosos apologized to their astonished guests, telling them that a substantial plumbing disaster threatened the Inn and that they needed to return home immediately.

"Well, let's have more champagne, everyone," bawled the red-eyed Alan as the reduced party of six struggled to get back into the spirit of the evening.

The celebration felt uncomfortable without the Generosos present, but everyone else tried to be merry and make small talk. Todd reckoned Alan must have been celebrating before they arrived, and Karen noticed the Winstons seemed older—much older—as if they were under stress or drinking too much.

After dinner was served and the singing waiter finally stopped throttling Neapolitan arias, the Bonners and Jewells bantered madly back and forth, as if there might be an embarrassing gap in the conversation. The Birthday Girl got louder, the Jewells' laughter became raucous, and the Winstons, eager to leave, remained mute. Just as they finished dessert, the maître d' arrived to thank everyone for choosing Jean Jacques and asked if he could do anything before the evening concluded.

"Bring the bill to Alan, quickly!" cried Karen Jewell, now grinning and wavering, pointing towards Alan, who looked like a drunken clown about to wobble out of his chair.

"Better give it to me," said Betsy the Birthday Girl, giving the maître d' a big wink. Uneasy laughter followed as the others folded their napkins, readying themselves for a speedy exit. "Any more champagne?" Betsy asked, then burped while everyone laughed.

Their waiter arrived, smiled, placed the bill on the table, and thanked the party again for choosing Jean Jacques. When

Betsy opened the leather wallet, she uttered a short groan and clasped her chest. Alan gave her an odd look while the rest gazed downwards, fiddled with their clothing, or pretended to check their watches.

"Well, guys, here's the bad news," announced Betsy. "We seem to have broken the—" she stopped and reread the bill. "Jesus! Three twenty-five-dollar martinis and a hundred-forty-five dollars' worth of Beluga caviar? Who?" She stopped again, staring at Alan. "Did *you* have all this? Well, *did* you?"

Alan nodded, blushed, and grinned. "Guess so."

Betsy's hands trembled as she held the bill up before Alan. "Guess so? *Guess* so?" Betsy began to cry. "You had all *this before we* even *got* here?"

Alan's face flushed redder, and his smirk vanished. "Well, what of it?" Silence. He grinned again, but nobody was watching.

"What of it?" screamed Betsy. "What *of* it?" She slammed the bill down on the table. "Well, I didn't get *any* caviar, and *I'm* the Birthday Girl!"

Jim Winston raised his hand in a gesture of silence. "We're all happy to chip in and help, aren't we?"

"Chip in?" shouted Betsy. "Well, *someone* better chip in, all right. We're looking at about sixteen hundred bucks here, folks—excluding my husband's little extras."

The party gasped, then gaped at one another.

"We thought this was mostly on Mike and Mary Ann," said Todd calmly. "We can't afford—"

"Can't *afford*?" cried Betsy.

"Betsy, stop shouting," Alan screamed in a voice that summoned their waiter, immediately following the maître d'.

Glancing about the table, the maître d' looked concerned. "Is something wrong?"

★ ★ ★

Early the following day, the Generosos drove to the regional office of the Massachusetts State Lottery while Billy stayed behind to tend the Inn. As expected, there were several calls for Mary Ann and Mike throughout the morning from unidentified "friends" who declined to leave messages. Billy was on snoop alert and quickly dispatched these queries with the excuse that his parents had left for their first real vacation in years.

The following weekend, the county paper featured an item about local innkeepers winning the state lotto jackpot and their plans to, before their retirement at the end of the year, donate nearly everything to homeless shelters in America, as well as provide aid to the famine in Africa. "As friends and acquaintances have testified," the writer concluded, "the Generosos are always very generous."

Early Checkout

Todd Thompson was a chronic dreamer. His naiveté and progressively odd behavior at home and work had begun to trouble everyone: his parents, friends, and otherwise tolerant boss. At twenty-four, Todd still lived with his parents, reluctant to survive alone in the outside world. He did have one faithful supporter: Ellen, his long-time, optimistic girlfriend. "Todd's very smart with a good heart," she'd say. "One day, he'll do something that will amaze us all."

Todd worked in a Boston brokerage, but the business bored him. Managing other people's finances was frustrating and mind-deadening. His fierce ambition was to be a screenwriter—an auteur, a prosperous and powerful independent filmmaker. One day he'd show the world how good movies *should* be made. Most of Todd's heroes and role models, however, were dead, insane, incontinent, residing in rest homes, or resting in celebrity cemeteries.

"There are simply no good flicks anymore," Todd would complain to his family at dinner. "Over-cut, over-lit, over-budgeted, stupid stories played by witless actors, and besides, *nobody* can direct, and that's why nobody goes to the movies anymore."

Gerald and Mabel, Todd's parents, stared at one another and rolled their eyes.

"Hell, I'd rather stay home and watch *Gone with the Wind*. Now *there*, by God, is one they can't re-make and ruin!" Todd got up from the table. "Thanks for the grub, Mom. Gotta get back to work." Humming "Tara's Theme," he strolled upstairs to resume work on his latest screenplay.

"The boy's losing it," Gerald grumbled.

"My lord, he *still* lives in that fantasy world," Mabel whispered.

"Hey, Mom!" Todd called down from his bedroom. "Friday night's dish night down at the Lyceum. Wanna go catch a flick?" After the bedroom door closed came the all-too-familiar theme from "Laura."

"He *has* lost it," Gerald groaned.

"Gone with the wind," Mabel sighed.

Todd idolized one person vital to his vision. He needed this all-important figure from the golden age of cinema to help him produce and direct *his* screenplays, stories that would sell and fill the movie houses again. His hero was the legendary Harry Hennigan, the last and grandest of the old-time cinema giants. Hennigan was now secluded someplace in the hills of Hollywood, hiding from fans, lawyers, bill collectors, the press, and the world. With the universal smash of his first film forty-two years ago, Harry Hennigan began at the top—and has been working his way downwards ever since. Now, Todd's true destiny was to rescue Harry's career.

For years, Todd struggled to reach the elusive master with unfortunate results. Whenever he managed to contact Hennigan's old chums, the response was usually a sigh or the click of a telephone hang-up. Todd sent a barrage of letters, faxes, and e-mails to all of Hennigan's last-known addresses in his quest. Some of these got returned, but all of them went unanswered. Until one day, a surprise arrived. The type-written letter bore an unusual return address: "Occupant, 1313 N. Dennis Avenue, Hollywood, CA." Not suspecting who it could be, Todd opened the letter and sat down to read:

> *Dear Todd,*
>
> *I beg you to accept my apologies for this long silence. Your hunch that I might be getting discouraged is not as wrong as I would wish it to be. The years keep slipping by, my hopes are dashed, and although I refuse any idea of surrender, it is becoming harder to smile away the rejections and broken promises. That's why your generously optimistic letter of December is all the more welcome for its long delay in reaching me.*

For a moment, Todd assumed this might be an elaborate hoax. The letter continued:

> *The movies of my time, those glorious masterpieces we both admire and adore, now belong to yesterday. Yet, those old shows will endure—on television and home entertainment, for as long as an audience is willing to watch them. Now, I'm afraid the only venues left for me are cable TV in America and the art-house circuits abroad. Perhaps we can find genuine financing if we are prepared to go low budget.*
>
> *I long for your thoughts on all this, Todd. You seem to be an intelligent and thoughtful fellow, and I look forward to meeting you. Why not join me in New York, at the Algonquin, for a meal and a long talk?*
>
> *Again, my belated and sincerest thanks,*
> *Harry Hennigan (213) 809-3349*
> *P.S. If you wish to write, please always address me as OCCUPANT.*

Gerald and Mabel were in the living room when they heard their son ranting and running around upstairs over their heads.

"Should we call EMS?" Gerald asked, peering over his newspaper.

"I'll see what's going on, dear," she replied and got up from her chair.

"Mom! Dad!" came the shrieks of their son in delirium. "Harry wrote back. Can you believe it? Hennigan *needs* me!"

"That boy *has* truly lost it," Gerald sighed.

After reading the letter several times, Todd picked up the phone and dialed Ellen's number. "Hey, it's me. Guess what? *Harry* wrote back! Harry wrote to *me*, Ellen. He wants me to—"

"Read me the letter, Todd. I can't *wait* to hear what he says."

There was silence at the other end of the line when Todd had finished. "Well? What do you think?"

"Oh, how fabulous! You're on your way now, aren't you?"

* * *

That evening at dinner, Todd could hardly sit still; he hadn't stopped blabbering all afternoon.

"How much will the man pay you, Todd?" asked Gerald, giving his son a stony stare.

Todd sat speechless, not quite comprehending what he had just heard. "Sorry. I don't understand what you're asking, Dad."

"Not a difficult question, is it, Todd?" Gerald's eyes widened, and his voice grew louder. "I *asked*, how much is the man paying you?"

It was a trap. Todd thought a moment, shifted in his chair, then took a sip of water. "We haven't discussed that yet."

"Haven't *discussed* it?"

Mabel put down her knife and fork. "Gerald, why don't you give Todd a chance to—"

"Chance? Give Todd a *chance*?" Gerald threw down his napkin. "The boy is twenty-four, he still lives at home, hates his job, has no wife, ain't got diddly in his bank account, and still drives *your* car. Now, he wants to run off to *la-la-land* and *donate* his time to the illustrious Mr. Hennigan—or should I say, the *penniless* Mr. Hennigan."

Todd cleared his throat. "Dad, you don't know a darn thing about Harry Hennigan—"

Gerald slammed his fist on the dining room table, causing everyone to jump and the water glasses to jiggle. "You seem to forget, Todd, that as an attorney specializing in corporate finance, I am well informed on those who pay their bills and those who don't. As it happens, I represent a bank that once loaned quite a sum to the celebrated Mr. Hennigan, and they're still fighting to recover just a portion of what he owes. So, I guess I know what's what, don't I?"

★ ★ ★

Before the flight to New York, Todd had dinner with Ellen at their favorite restaurant to celebrate the forthcoming meeting with Hennigan and Todd's decision to move out of his parent's home and find a place of his own.

"I feel life is becoming more meaningful, Ellen," Todd said, sipping his wine.

"What did your parents say when you told them you were moving out?" Ellen asked, putting down her cocktail.

"Well, the old man suggested it in another of his extended lectures on the correct way to live my life. Like, isn't it high time you asked Ellen *the question*?"

"And your mom?"

"Well, just before I walked out, she gave me a thumbs-up."

Ellen raised her glass. "Well then, here's to the Todd Thompson and Harry Hennigan team."

Todd raised his glass and smiled. "And here's looking at you, kid."

★ ★ ★

A week later, Todd took a flight from Boston to La Guardia. That evening, when he arrived at the Algonquin, he found Harry Hennigan—all three hundred and twenty-two pounds of him—seated at a single table towards the rear of the dining room. Harry had already consumed enough appetizers sufficient for the main course.

"Todd, my good fellow!" Roaring like an elderly sea lion, Harry Hennigan struggled to his feet, extending his hand. "Welcome to the Algonquin, home of the Round Table: Parker, Woollcott, Benchley, Ferber—and now, the two of *us*! Come, seat yourself."

Todd took Harry's hand. Overcome, Todd's voice trembled. "Thank you, Master."

"Todd, old man, we have a big job ahead of us," Harry said, nearly out of breath, sitting down and pouring a glass of champagne each. "The money promised for my next project has been delayed, perhaps withdrawn, because of political unrest in Honduras—the usual banana republic stuff."

"I didn't know you got your money from—"

"Honduras?" Harry smiled. "Todd, we get our money from everywhere and anywhere these days. *Except for* America, that is."

"Why not here?"

"Back taxes," Harry said with a great grin. "The moment Uncle Sam finds a dollar in my bank—any bank—he takes it. Licensed larceny, I call it."

Todd fell silent, trying to reconcile what he'd just heard from Harry against his initial expectation—a *team*, writing and producing *together*. Now it seemed Harry only wanted Todd to help find funding.

"Todd, your expertise in high finance would be invaluable in securing much-needed capital. Perhaps you could give us some guidance?"

"Well, in my world, we require certain guarantees—."

At that moment, Todd was interrupted by the arrival of their waiter.

"Mr. Hennigan, would you like to hear the specials for the day?"

"Start with the soup-du-jour if you wouldn't mind. My young friend here has quite an appetite, and so do I."

"Very good, Mr. Hennigan," replied the waiter as Harry helped himself to another mammoth serving of crab cakes.

Listening to Harry's fantasies about film financing and the role he might be expected to play, Todd's appetite began to wane. Todd realized there was no way he could get a penny for Harry Hennigan. Without thinking, Harry himself had revealed the terrible truth. Todd spent a restless night in his overheated room at the Mayflower Hotel, confused by Harry's bizarre notions about business and angry that they had never once discussed Todd's scripts or ideas for a collaborative venture.

He waited for Harry in the lobby until nine-thirty. They had agreed to meet for breakfast at nine, but when Harry didn't show up, Todd went to the front desk to ask if someone could ring Mr. Hennigan's room.

"I'm sorry, sir, but Mr. Hennigan checked out early this morning."

"But we were supposed to have breakfast together at nine."

The clerk walked over to a row of mailboxes and retrieved a small envelope from one of the mail slots. "Are you Todd?" the clerk asked.

"Yes, I am."

"This is for you."

The clerk handed Todd the envelope and waited for him to open it. Todd turned his back to the clerk, opened the envelope, and withdrew a note.

Todd, my good fellow!
Forgive my abrupt departure. I am in difficult circumstances that require my immediate attention at home. I'll ring you when things have settled down.

Thanks for your understanding and for coming to New York. Remember, old boy. We've got a big job ahead of us. Keep swinging!
   Love, Harry.

★ ★ ★

There were no calls or letters from Harry for several weeks. Feeling betrayed, Todd became depressed. In the meantime, he and Ellen found an apartment in Cambridge and decided to set up 'housekeeping together,' as he described it to his mother one day when his father was out of the house.

"Does this mean you're getting married, Todd?" asked the optimistic Mabel, whose abiding faith in her peculiar son often drove her husband into a fury.

"No, Mom, and please don't start counting your grandchildren before they hatch."

"Well, Ellen's a nice girl, Todd. You could have done worse."

"Thanks, Mom, you're a peach."

"That's what your father used to say to me before we were married."

★ ★ ★

Several weeks after Harry Hennigan's hasty departure from the Algonquin, Todd got out of the shower and found a brief message on his cell phone that made his entire body quiver.

"Todd, it's Harry. Sorry not to have called you sooner, but I am deep in a desperate situation. No, I'm not drunk—and I have a witness beside me who will attest to my sobriety. Anyway, please call me tonight. We have much to discuss."

When Ellen came home that night, Todd played her the message. "Wow, Todd. He sounds like the voice of doom."

"I suppose he'll want you to go out and see him." Ellen opened a bag of groceries and began moving vegetables into the fridge.

"You think I shouldn't?"

"I think he's a bit weird, Todd."

"Who knows? Anyway, we'll see what he wants tonight." Todd sat silently for a few moments. "Feel sorry for the old guy, Ellen. Life hasn't been easy for him, has it?"

"Seems Harry has become his own worst enemy. Walking out on you in New York was not cool."

Todd sat and thought for a moment. "I just wanted to give the old guy a hand. He hasn't got too many friends left, and maybe not many years left either." A tear-filled Todd's eye and ran down his cheek.

Ellen walked over to Todd and put her arms around him. "I knew you wouldn't desert him, Todd. That's why I love you."

"My parents think I'm a fool."

"Perhaps you are," Ellen said, stroking his hair, "but now and then, we all need to forge ahead and take risks. So, tonight, we'll drink again to the team of Thompson and Hennigan. The world is waiting for your sunrise, Todd."

Todd looked up at Ellen and grinned. "And here's looking at you, kid."

★ ★ ★

When he'd finished his call that evening with Harry, Todd told Ellen that Harry had found an Iranian banker who swore he'd do anything to help Harry get back on his feet, and Harry wanted Todd to be at their first meeting. Todd knew he had no alternative.

"I said I'd go to L.A. and do this thing. Harry promised to pay my airfare, but he can't pay me a fee."

"Go for it," Ellen said. "You only live twice."

On Friday of that week, Ellen drove Todd to Boston's Logan Airport, dropped him off at Terminal E, kissed him goodbye, and wished him bon voyage. When Todd entered the terminal, he didn't notice the morning newspaper headlines with

Hennigan's photo on the front page. Nor did he pay attention to the large, wide-screen television monitors showing clips of Hennigan's films with countless celebrities being interviewed about Harry's career.

Todd went straight to check-in, displayed his ticket, deposited one piece of luggage, picked up a boarding pass, and sat down far away from all the TV monitors. Todd wanted his privacy now—a chance to read over his best script ever and to dream how he and Harry Hennigan would, one day, make beautiful movies together.

Her SweetBerry

Jumping out of a creamy-yellow Porsche Boxster and racing up the steps to her preppy East Hampton cottage, Kathy Watson bounced in the front door and dropped her oversized Gucci handbag onto a chair. Greeting her husband with a strident "Ta-da!" Kathy raised her arm triumphantly, gripping an object in her clenched hand.

Kevin Watson—sallow, slim, and far too old for forty—glanced up from his *Wall Street Journal*. "You've finally gotten a raise?"

"Nope." Kathy grinned and wiggled the concealed object before him, her red hair shivering with expectancy. "Guess again."

Kevin put down the paper and snorted. "You won the lottery? Nope, Auntie Agnes died and left us a fortune? Hey, you've bought me a new digital camera, right?"

"Well, not quite. Kevin, look what they gave me at work." Kathy opened her hand, revealing a small, green shell-shaped gadget: two bulbous buttons protruding from the outer casing resembled the eyes of a frightened frog.

"Well! You now own an ugly little green clamshell—with eyeballs." Kevin snorted again and returned to the Journal.

"No, dummy, it's a *SweetBerry*!"

"OK, so *what* does it do, or shouldn't I ask?"

"Look, Kevin, I can get all my e-mails on this little gadget—anytime, anyplace. It has a camera, an all-format music player, and full Internet connectivity. Also, a buzzer and a vibrator, so

I always know when *I've got mail*."

"And a *vibrator* as well. Say! Who'd be without one?" Kevin huffed, burying his face in the paper. "So, it works *anywhere*?"

"Yup. Worldwide, twenty-four-seven."

"But what happens if you're in the bathroom?"

Kathy sat down on the armrest next to him, looking puzzled. "What do you mean?"

"Well, does it talk to you while doing private things? Does it go off in bed as well?"

Kathy playfully whacked Kevin's shoulder. "Don't be a moron. My SweetBerry keeps me fully connected—no need for a computer."

"Well, I hope it helps you remember appointments better."

"Like what?"

"Like we're due at the Tully's for dinner—in about a half-hour."

"Oh, damn! I almost forgot."

"Not to worry, dear. Little SweetBerry is here; all will be well."

"Very funny. Come on, help me pick out a dress. Which car are we taking?"

Kevin shrugged his shoulders. "The Mercedes is low on gas. Better take yours."

★ ★ ★

Being late for the dinner party, Kathy absentmindedly dropped the live SweetBerry into her handbag and hurried to get dressed. Dinner for eight was underway when they arrived, but the Tullys, naturally easy-going and always good-humored, didn't mind. "Good to see you both," chirped Jane Tully, leading the Watsons into the dining room. "Where've you guys been hiding?"

"Kevin's been tied up on weekends at work, and I've been traveling," Kathy replied.

"And we're still redoing the basement, so life's been hectic," added Kevin.

"God, it's a wonder the Watsons *ever* get any time off," Jane babbled, passing the breadbasket. "Well, dive in—there's plenty to eat."

"Yeah, I even managed to leave you a morsel or two," chuckled the fleshy and ever-jolly Tom Tully. *Who says fat men aren't happy?* Mused Kevin while Tom thrust a large silver serving platter loaded with butter-covered vegetables under his nose.

Breem. Breem.

"What's that?" Jane cried, startled.

Breem. Breem.

Kathy's face reddened as she reached down and rummaged through her handbag. All conversation stopped.

"Sorry," Kathy said. "My machine is calling me."

"What?" grinned Tom, leaning dangerously over Kathy's décolleté. "You didn't tell us you brought a *guest*."

A brief quiver of laughter around the table didn't relieve Kathy's embarrassment as she dug for the SweetBerry.

Breem! Breem!

"Sounds like *someone's* getting impatient," Jane exclaimed in a shrill trill. "Well, let's adjourn to the living room for coffee, shall we?"

When the dinner guests rose to leave, Kathy retrieved the SweetBerry and browsed the blue-green screen before clicking one of the bulging eyeballs to *Off*.

"So, what the hell did it say?" Kevin whispered, picking at his mustache.

"Welcome from SweetBerry. We hope you enjoy your new connectivity." Jane looked up at Kevin. "Guess I don't need this at parties."

"Or anywhere else," Kevin glared at the open clamshell, which now appeared to be staring back.

Kathy laughed and plopped the SweetBerry back into her

handbag. "C'mon," she said, grabbing Kevin's arm. "Let's join the others."

★ ★ ★

While Kevin and Kathy were getting ready for bed, it happened again.

Breem. Breem.

"I don't believe it," Kevin cried, pulling on his pajamas.

Kathy reached over to her night table, opened the clamshell cover, and scrolled rapidly down the screen to look at her latest message. *Hey, Kathy! Wouldn't you like some warm milk before bed?* The text rolled over an animated background of milky mustaches.

"I don't believe it either," mumbled Kathy, reading the message to herself.

"Well, who's it from?"

"That's what's weird. It's not signed. It's a kind of welcome note from *your friendly SweetBerry.*"

"Haven't you gotten any *real* e-mails—like from work?"

"Not yet," Kathy said.

"OK, let's get some sleep, shall we? And for god's sake, shut that damn thing off or put it downstairs where we can't hear it."

Kathy picked up the SweetBerry and took it to the kitchen, where the battery charger sat waiting on a countertop. She coupled the charger to the SweetBerry, watched the green charger light winking, picked up a box of macadamia nut cookies, turned back upstairs, then stopped momentarily to stare at the SweetBerry, which had shifted itself into a kind of kneeling position on the counter. Puzzled, she stopped and waited. Then, refusing to look back, she hurried up to the bedroom.

★ ★ ★

The next day, Kevin and Kathy decided to escape household chores and work worries and spend the afternoon by the pool. Kathy received several irritating messages from the office on her SweetBerry. Desperate for a peaceful day at home, she left the device indoors. But they had hardly settled into their poolside chairs when a furious mechanical shrieking erupted inside the house.

"Jesus, Kathy. Is that your SweetBerry?"

Kathy jumped up from her chair. "It must be."

"It's screaming, for god's sake! Why is it so loud?"

Grabbing her beach bathrobe, Kathy bolted barefoot toward the back door. "I don't *know*, Kevin," she shouted. "I'll try to stop it." In the kitchen, Kathy was astonished to see the SweetBerry standing up on edge, as if alive. What she read on the screen made her skin crawl: *You left me. Where are you?*

Feeling nauseous and a bit panicky, Kathy quickly deleted the message. Convinced she better not tell Kevin what she had seen, she slipped the SweetBerry into her bathrobe pocket and returned to the pool.

★ ★ ★

The rest of the day passed uneventfully, and following a peaceful afternoon at the poolside, the Watsons decided to buy lobsters for dinner. Kevin commented on how quiet the SweetBerry had been on their way back from the supermarket. "I may have to keep it with me at night," Kathy said, knowing Kevin would object.

"Whatever keeps the little bastard quiet," Kevin said, turning into their drive. He parked the car and turned off the engine.

Breem. Breem.

"See, you offended him!" Kathy laughed.

"Him? Who said it was a *he*? Maybe it's a *girl*."

Kathy studied the screen, scrolling slowly through a message from her boss. "Carl has signed a new client and wants me at work early Monday morning to get things started. He suggests I might get a head start and send him a preliminary assessment by Sunday night."

"But that's *tomorrow*! You *promised* not to work weekends," Kevin said, jerking the car door open.

"Kevin, when Carl makes a suggestion, it's a *command*, and he expects it done *yesterday*."

"I thought he was on vacation."

"He is—in the Bahamas."

"How does he—?" Kevin stopped. "Naturally," he muttered in a soft tone. "He's got a SweetBerry."

"Yup...and his has full Internet capability, plus the whole suite of online office tools and remote printing and storage and . . ."

"Of course!" Kevin shouted. "Now, nobody *ever* gets any peace, twenty-four-seven, holidays, weekends, Caribbean vacations, whatever." Kevin leaped out of the car and slammed the door shut. "I'll bet he's got it with him even when he's taking a crap."

"Kevin, calm down. You're being ridiculous."

"No, *you're* the one who's being ridiculous, coddling that stupid little widget like it's your child, for god's sake."

"It's *not* my child; it's a business tool."

"It's a *toy*, and you know it. Let's get something straight: I am *not* having that damn thing ruin our lifestyle, so the next time it goes off will be the last, I promise. We had an *agreement*, Kathy, remember?"

Kathy got out of the car, gathered her bundles, and stomped into the house. Once inside, she dropped the groceries on the kitchen countertop, reached inside her handbag for the SweetBerry, and opened it. Looking about to see if Kevin was watching, Kathy scrutinized the screen. She was astounded by what appeared: A moving mass of red and black waves in the background roiling in stormy turbulence, out of which a liquid-like hand with long bony tendrils was beckoning.

"Couldn't wait, could you?"

Kathy jumped as the SweetBerry hit the floor and skidded under the table. "Shit, Kevin, you scared the hell out of me." She knelt to retrieve the unharmed instrument.

"Tough little bugger, isn't it?" Kevin noticed that Kathy was sweating, her hand trembling as she attempted to retrieve the fallen SweetBerry. "Hey Kath, I'm sorry. I didn't mean to frighten you."

"Never mind," Kathy said, rising to her feet and placing the SweetBerry back on the countertop. "The SweetBerry helps me work out of the office; I'd hoped more time at home would be good for us."

"I know," Kevin said, putting an arm around her shoulder. "But now, you're getting weird about this widget. Can't you leave it for just *one* day?"

That evening at dinner, Kathy and Kevin agreed there would be no more arguments about the SweetBerry; the machine would be turned off at mealtime. Before their trial separation a year ago, they had often argued about time spent at work versus time spent together. There had been too many loud disagreements. From now on, weekends and the evening meal would be sacrosanct.

* * *

Preparing for bed that evening, Kathy seemed puzzled that her SweetBerry wasn't working correctly. Kevin assured her that the "poor little gadget" just needed a rest and a good night's recharging—like people, he added with a wink. Kevin turned out the lights and instantly fell asleep.

At one a.m., it came—like a herd of banshees—a savage screaming from the kitchen that catapulted both Kathy and Kevin out of bed in seconds. Each fumbled for bedside light switches.

"I'll go," Kathy shouted, forgetting her slippers as she fumbled for the door handle. She ran to the staircase and gripped the handrail after stubbing her toe in the darkened hallway. Kathy could hear Kevin cursing from the bedroom and knew he was losing it.

Kathy raced into the kitchen, stopped, and stared in disbelief. Her SweetBerry crawled about the granite countertop like an enraged spider greedy for prey. Its green plastic shell shimmered and blinked fiercely, the screen flaming with red and yellow liquid lava-like images. Kevin appeared in the doorway, shaking his head in disbelief.

"What's wrong with this damn thing?" cried Kathy, picking up the SweetBerry and shaking it furiously. "This can't be happening; it *can't*."

BREEM! BREEM! BREEM!

Kevin lunged forward, snatched the screaming SweetBerry from Kathy's hand, and charged out the back door.

"Kevin, where are you going?"

"Not to worry, Kathy. The poor little thing's thirsty and needs a drink."

"What the hell are you talking about, Kevin?" shouted Kathy, chasing after him.

"I know about these things, Kathy," Kevin cried out, unlatching the gate on the fence surrounding their pool. "Believe me, darling, I know about thirst and being deprived. Don't worry, honey. Daddy will sort out our naughty little boy, won't he?"

The automatic outdoor lights came on, filling the back gardens and pool area with frosty tubular beams perforating the evening mist. Kathy watched Kevin hovering awkwardly at the end of the pool by the diving board. He was rocking back and forth, grinning maniacally at the SweetBerry cradled in his right hand.

"Kevin, *no!*" Kathy watched in horror as Kevin wound up like a baseball player and pitched the SweetBerry straight toward the pool's center. It hit the water with a small plop. Kevin stood at the edge of the pool, rocking back and forth, laughing like a giddy little boy, waving *bye-bye* to the now-submerged SweetBerry.

Kathy stood back from the pool, terrified by what might happen next. As the outdoor lights dimmed, she began to panic. It was getting colder by the minute. The pool assumed a dark-green iridescence—dim and murky at first, then growing brighter and more garish, blazing like neon tubes in an amusement park. A foul smell filled the air as Kevin snorted and coughed, repeatedly trying to clear his throat.

Then, like a toilet flushing, the pool water gurgled, churned, and swirled while Kevin stood petrified—the stench of burning plastic filling the air. Gasping for air, Kevin reached out clumsily for the ladder next to the diving board, but before he could take hold of it, he stumbled forward and fell into the foul green vortex of roiling water, water reaching out to suck him down into its turbulent core.

"Oh *god!*" Kathy screamed, running towards the pool. "Kevin? *Kevin!*"

Kevin sat up and switched on the bedside table lamp. "Kathy, wake up!" he yelled, reaching over to stop her from thrashing about the bed. Breathing heavily, Kathy was conscious in a few seconds, her hair matted and snarled, her pale face drawn and clammy.

"Wow, you've never done *that* before," Kevin exclaimed, stroking her damp hair.

"Done what?" mumbled Kathy, trying to untangle herself from the bedclothes.

"You were yelling in your sleep. Look—you've pulled all the sheets off."

Kathy shivered, forcing a wan smile. "I had a terrible dream: You threw the SweetBerry into the pool, and then you drowned."

Kevin lay back and sighed. "It's two-thirty; let's try and get back to sleep, OK? We'll discuss your SweetBerry's future in the morning." He switched off the bedside lamp, groaned, rolled about, and pulled the covers over his head.

* * *

The following day after breakfast, Kathy took the SweetBerry into her office to check for messages and was relieved to discover that everything seemed normal; two e-mails from her boss and a cheery note from a friend who had just gotten a SweetBerry. Suddenly, Kathy heard the back door slam shut, followed by Kevin stomping about the house. He was banging doors and talking to himself. Kathy left the office and stepped into the kitchen, her pulse pounding.

"You won't believe this, but the Mercedes has *four* flat tires," Kevin shouted, tearing through pages in the phone book. "I'll have to call the goddam garage or get a hand pump. It's unbelievable."

"Were they slashed? Nobody can even get *into* our garage, can they?"

"I can't see how," Kevin said. "The garage doors were locked. This is crazy."

That evening at dinner, Kathy and Kevin had their worst fight ever. After breakfast the next day, Kevin stormed out of the house in a fury, scraping the passenger side door of his Mercedes against the garage in his rush to leave. Later that morning, Kevin called to say he'd had it out with his boss, who told him he no longer had a job.

"What did you *do*, for god's sake?" Kathy asked, not wanting to hear his answer.

"You'll laugh when I tell you," Kevin replied.

"I doubt it—try me."

"My company requires that *everyone* carry a SweetBerry from now on. Isn't that funny, Kath? Isn't that just so unbelievably hilarious? Ha! I told Bill where he could stick his SweetBerry. Ha! Ha! I don't hear you laughing, Kath. Why aren't you laughing?"

After eleven, the hospital phoned to tell Kathy that Kevin had put his fist through a plate-glass window at the office and had badly severed a major artery. Feeling curiously unmoved, Kathy told the nurse she'd be there in the morning and hung up.

* * *

That night, alone and miserable, Kathy opened a fresh pint of her favorite ice cream—macadamia toffee swirl—and withdrew into her office, closing and locking the door behind her. Picking up the SweetBerry, she quickly scanned the message screen. What she read did not come as a complete surprise:

> *Dear Kathy,*
> *Now that we're alone, I've been meaning to chat. Kevin's been under much stress lately. Why not go out tonight and buy him a nice big bottle of gin?*
> *Love,*
> *Your SweetBerry*

You Can Bank on It

Ted Thayer, a successful health insurance executive, but regarded as an outsider by village locals, lived by himself with his adopted rescue basset hounds in a Tudor mansion overlooking Lake Neshoba in Centerville, Pennsylvania. Ted took early retirement and a substantial severance while suffering from heart disease in his late fifties. Following the unexpected death of his wife, Kathy, Ted's meager social life ended. Most in Centerville knew only of his temper and heavy drinking. After Kathy passed, townspeople avoided him altogether, leaving Ted to spend his final days in solitude, caring for his hounds and the estate.

One afternoon, driving home from a walk in the woods with his dogs, Ted noticed a sign posted outside a modest, wisteria-covered cottage on the edge of town: B*ank-Owned—For Sale—Doyle Realty*, and underneath, *By Appointment Only*. Ted thought the sign peculiar; Centerville was a desirable and affluent town, even during hard times. Upon inquiry at the real estate office, the agent told Ted the cottage belonged to a senior woman who was ill. Her health insurance had run out, and she could no longer pay the mortgage.

"What will happen to her?" Ted asked, noting the man's nervous need to make a deal.

"She'll go to a retirement home," the agent replied. "Anyway, it's a fair price and a fine property. Are you interested?"

When Ted asked the woman's name, the agent revealed the asking price yet declined to disclose her identity. "I can always look it up in the phone book," Ted said, getting up to leave.

"OK," the agent replied. "It's Lillian Merwin. She has lived in Centerville all her life."

Returning home, Ted opened the front door, let the bassets out, and, leaving the door ajar, walked straight to the living room and mixed himself a cocktail. He slumped into his leather recliner to ponder, nursing a bourbon, until nightfall. The discovery of the woman's name brought down a tumble of childhood memories: Mrs. Merwin had been his piano teacher as a boy, and although he desperately wanted to play, he had little talent. For years she encouraged him, reminding Ted that one must never quit if one wished to succeed. Ted's parents thought his piano instruction a waste of time and money, yet he always went happily to his weekly lessons. Holding those thoughts, Ted fell fast asleep in the darkening lounge, the hounds resting at his feet.

The next day, Ted returned to the office of Doyle Realty and told the agent he would pay off the note—on the condition that his identity remained anonymous. At first, the agent hesitated, but as Ted offered ten thousand dollars over the asking price, he agreed. Lillian Merwin would keep her house, and the bank would cancel its foreclosure.

★ ★ ★

Several months after securing Lillian Merwin's home, Ted Thayer suffered a fatal heart attack. His only living relatives—his sister, Ellen, and a brother-in-law—descended upon his estate with avarice. Still, after hearing the will, Ellen was appalled to discover that Ted had left most of his assets to animal rescue agencies. She would receive ten thousand dollars. Not one penny more.

"He must have been mad," she screeched. "I'll contest the will." The attorneys advised Ellen to take the money and scurry. Otherwise, she would lose it all in hopeless pursuit.

In his will, Ted stipulated a memorial service at the Episcopal Church in Centerville. "All the music," he specified, "must be by Bach—my favorite composer—whose works I could never play. Should my hounds survive me, I have arranged for a good foster home. Everything has been paid for in advance, including my marble mausoleum."

After the funeral, Ellen remarked how only a few old folks attended the memorial. "Undoubtedly, he will not be remembered with kindness," she said. "And who was that little old lady with the funny purple pillbox hat and white gloves sitting in the front pew?" Nobody seemed to know. Ellen and her husband left the church to return home, and Ted was transported to his final resting place...unaccompanied.

A week later, Ellen returned to Centerville to settle some final business and collect her inheritance. Before departing, though, she and her husband drove out to the cemetery. They had no difficulty finding Ted's gravesite on a hillock overlooking a few dozen modest headstones and were astonished by the massive sepulcher he had erected in his memory.

Ellen was also surprised to see fresh flowers at the base of his grave. "I suppose he arranged to have a florist do this each week, didn't he? And with *that* horror," she hissed, shaking a reproving finger at his burial chamber, "Ted has assured himself a perpetual position in Centerville."

"He certainly enjoyed wasting his money," her husband replied while they got back into their car.

But it was Ted's epitaph that troubled them the most, and they both pondered it on their lonely ride home together.

"My soul, and my lucre, now belong to the orphaned animals of this world," he had written. "I hope to find all of them in heaven, but none of you."

Night Riders

They crouched together like endless rows of tilting tombstones, reposing somberly, one behind the other, far into the horizon—ravaged hulks huddled under the desert twilight, clutched nose-to-tail, and wing-to-wing, clinging haplessly to their rusty remains. By nightfall, history had turned another silent page over these voiceless hundreds, and every evening each waited in their suffering—waited for them—those dreaded birds.

In the daytime, soft winds swept waves of hot sand carelessly over their rotting tires that stank like old shoes—footgear long past usefulness. A callous sun glared down upon blackened cockpit windows looking like oversized aviator's goggles but devoid of pilots' eyes and heads. At one time—gallant, sleek, and shiny—now deposed and darkened by dust and neglect, the elderly squatted without noses or tails, displaying filthy body parts, gaping cabins, stripped wheel gears decapitated and discarded. The once-powerful stood sulking, horrid herds of infirmed elephants huddled in the Bone Yard, deprived of their former supremacy and prestige.

    Throughout the Bone Yard, loose flaps creaked and screeched in anguish. A tire squealed and exhaled. An occasional cabin door fell open and banged itself repeatedly, witlessly. After a short silence, a battered propeller squeaked, groaned, and expired, dropping silently into the sand. By day's end, the guards will drive home and be with their families, leaving the Bone Yard gated and unattended. As the sun disappeared in a green flash over the horizon, an evening breeze sprang up carrying faint voices, restless moans, and frequent sighs, a gruesome gathering of mourners at the graveside.

Just before the moonrise, a new gust sprang up, cooling the fragrant air, now redolent of sweet cactus and desert rose. Then, the birds came—hundreds of them: Vultures, ravens, hawks, screeching and circling, roosting rudely on rusty wings, tails, and split-bellies, releasing their droppings as loathsome reminders that *they*, after all, were still flying. Flocks descended, perched, and became still—anthracite statues staring mirthlessly into the desert dusk.

The Bone Yard became mute; there was no conversation; nobody was awake. Suddenly, there were low murmurs.

"I want to go *now* . . . it's my turn." It was Jonah, a silvery hulk, a Constellation Starliner, once the pride of TWA. Jonah tried looking about, but could not move an inch.

"You wanted to go last month," rumbled Buff, a decrepit B-52 Stratofortress bomber about to lose a wing. "Why don't you just go?"

"I'm afraid," came the whispered reply.

"Of *what*, knucklehead?" Buff was in a bad temper tonight, and everyone knew it. B-52s were often this way; they understood that nothing was for them beyond the Bone Yard. Only last week, a group of bomber pilots had toured the Yard looking for their old planes, and when they left, some were crying.

"My old captain found me last week," Jonah replied eagerly. "He said we'd fly again, and soon. I knew we would."

The Bone Yard remained hushed, and then Buff spoke. Buff was the most senior, and the group respected his understanding. "No pilot will come, Jonah—you'll have to do it alone, just like the rest of us, and remember, you've got one shot at it. So, go and have a wonderful ride. We'll be waiting to hear all about it."

"Like stories around a campfire," crackled a dust-shrouded Boeing 377, listing on its flat left wheel.

Gradually, an odd choir of hollow voices rose in harmony, some quivering and coughing, others strong and committed, and a few so decrepit they could hardly speak, but each had their say.

"All we want is one more."

"Why have they left us here? We can still make it."

"I am . . . I'm strong enough."

"Others went back; we want to go too."

A few did make it back up, only one more time—one final ride, just for the memories. People on the ground could hear them, it was said, but not everyone. These rides happened only at night, and although no one ever really saw them, hearing the familiar overhead rumble of those old engines was enough for the pilots, their families, and occasional friends who, if they didn't believe, were kind enough to pretend.

Some air-traffic controllers did hear them—first, the radio identifiers, always beginning in sporadic gasps of ancient Morse code, fading in and out of the ether, a few dots and dashes crying out to ask if anyone was listening:

"Hello, hello, hello . . . do you copy?"

No images appeared on their glowing green and blue radar screens; no reports were filed. Although not everyone believed, the old-timers knew well enough and remained silent. It was *their* time—private moments with tears and flecks of memories.

★ ★ ★

A week later, on a strangely bright and star-filled night, after the guards left and the birds had gone to sleep, Jonah summoned his courage and declared he would go next: tomorrow night, for sure, no more waiting, no further excuses. Buff and the others were elated, relieved that Jonah would finally have his moment, and they'd all be there waiting. They would be ready to hear the story, eager to share every detail of his journey, from take-off to landing.

Early the following day, just at sunrise, when the guards returned and the gates opened, a small green utility truck carrying workers wearing sunglasses and hardhats and hauling heavy tools sputtered across the Yard and parked beside Jonah. In that tragic, unspoken moment, his comrades realized that old Jonah had, indeed, waited one day too many.

Old Thompson

The scoffers around town mocked Old Thompson and ridiculed him, for every year, he reiterated the same old tale: Pudding, his long-lost yellow Labrador, would return on Christmas Eve. Long ago, Pudding disappeared during a furious blizzard the day before Christmas. When Old Thompson searched for him, he became lost, suffered frostbite, and nearly succumbed to the cold. Caleb Turner, a neighbor, heard the old man's cries and found him wandering in the woods half-frozen. Turner dragged him home and made him some tea. When Old Thompson, with a fever, attempted to go back outdoors, Caleb restrained him and called the doctor.

★ ★ ★

Hobbling into Miller's grocery store on Christmas Eve, Old Thompson closed the door, turned, smiled, waved, and offered salutations to the group gathered about an iron coal stove, savoring their hot cider. They greeted him as *Old Thompson*; none remembered his real name.

"Have you come for Pudding's Christmas treats?" cried Amy Miller, retrieving dog-bone biscuits from a shelf where she always kept a box for Old Thompson.

Old Thompson mumbled *yes, thank you*, then reached for his wallet with trembling hands.

"It's on the house," Amy said, dropping the biscuits into a bag.

"Probably gives 'em to the birds," a villager murmured.

"Or eats them himself," someone muttered.

Shuffles and titters followed.

"Pudding will be back this Christmas!" Old Thompson shouted, shaking his biscuits, defying the world.

"Of course he will," whispered Amy, comforting the old man and smoothing his wrinkles. "Now, drive safely, old man, and a Merry Christmas to you—and Pudding."

When the group raised their mugs, Old Thompson raised his bag of biscuits and then stopped. "And Pudding wishes everyone...." The group sat and watched; a few looked down or away. "Can't remember what I was going to say." A tear slipped down his cheek as he turned away and shuffled towards the door.

"Take care, old man," someone called.

Clutching his biscuits, Old Thomson departed the store, leaving the door ajar. The villagers shook their heads and returned to their cider and chatter, leaving Old Thompson to the wind and his solitude.

★ ★ ★

When dusk dropped, and the sky vanished, Caleb Turner watched Old Thompson arrive in his ancient Ford, slam the door, and shuffle three steep steps toward his bungalow. After bumbling the latch, he slowly came to a stop. Calling for Pudding, he looked out over the starless blackness before entering his house, closing the door loudly behind him.

Caleb told his wife that Old Thompson was not wearing a hat, scarf, or mittens, but he was home, safe.

The night dripped, silent as an icicle, and then a few snowflakes pin-wheeled to the ground. Inside his musty, dust-layered bungalow, Old Thompson switched on a lamp and knelt to ignite the gas fire, leaving the gift of dog biscuits on the floor. Dinner tonight would be grand indeed: fried calves' liver with bacon, onions, and mushrooms, but Pudding would have only the liver.

"It's Christmas, you know," Old Thompson called out, opening a can of mushrooms, "and if no one else wants these mushrooms, I'll eat 'em all!" His laugh shivered the room like a gust of winter wind. "Something else, Pudding. Wait 'til you see what I've got!"

* * *

With dinner cooked and served, Old Thompson sat alone at his worn kitchen table—feeding himself with one hand, handing down scraps with the other—watching a wintry kaleidoscope churn against the windows. Then he rose, beckoned Pudding to follow, and limped into the living room.

Resting in a threadbare chair with a glass of port, Old Thompson felt happier than he had in years. Weary of tears and lonely hours, he vowed to rejoin the world again. Tomorrow, Christmas Day, he and Pudding would go to town to buy more biscuits and watch the children meet Santa Claus in the village square, as they always did. Folks would be so pleased to see them together.

It was now midnight. Pudding lay at the old man's feet, having enjoyed his share of the liver and a large helping of biscuits. Old Thompson leaned over, stroked the dog's back and ears, and thanked him for the best Christmas ever. Exhausted, both were soon fast asleep.

* * *

Caleb Turner told his wife that he had not seen Old Thompson leave his house for two days. "Better go check—I'll be right back."

He found Old Thompson in his chair—eyes wide open, baring a toothless smile. At his feet rested a bowl and a half-empty bag of dog-bone biscuits. The gas fire, long expired, had left the house stone cold. Caleb found frozen white paw prints leading to and from the bungalow that he never mentioned to anyone, not even his wife.

When the villagers heard the news a few days later, they shook their heads, as they had done a hundred times before. Amy Miller wept, for she knew Old Thompson had spent the last of his savings on the finest calves' liver a dog could want.

Beasley's Machines

- Dedicated to Record Producer R. Peter Munves -

Raymond Eliot Beasley—his wife Ellen frequently summoned the full name—sat alone in the attic playing old records in his dust-webbed playground, surrounded by shelves groaning under hundreds of platters, each meticulously sorted and alphabetically annotated. Mr. Beasley also collected hefty antique players with brass horns (*Victrolas*), but they also had gathered time's ashes both around and inside them.

"Can't buy new needles any longer," Ellen warned. "Next spring, it's off to the dump with the entire lot. *All* of them."

"They're priceless!" wailed the horrified Mr. Beasley.

"Come spring, out they go."

"Out *you'll* go!" cried the bug-eyed Mr. Beasley, clutching Paul Whiteman to his bosom. "My friends are all *here*."

"They all died decades ago, Beasley." Ellen coughed, shaking a duster in his face. "Dust to dust, you know."

"These are my *time* machines," protested the anguished Mr. Beasley.

"It's time these machines *disappeared*," came the retort.

* * *

Each night, following dinner, Mr. Beasley rose to his heavenly eaves. Ellen could hear the spring-ring of the loft ladder, with mutters and dull foot-thumps overhead, then the Victrola's creaky hand crank, followed by a few minutes of muffled music.

In warm weather, Mr. Beasley opened the skylight to his star-spangled inky way while the platters played *The Old Oaken Bucket* and ghosts sang to the dreams of his childhood.

When You've Come to the End of a Perfect Day concluded each evening's musicale.

"Close that skylight when you come down," Ellen shouted. "And remember, next week we're cleaning house."

"You'll go as well," growled the unregenerate Mr. Beasley, placing another platter on the worn, green-felt turntable. "I have a good mind to get up and fly right out of that skylight. *Tonight!*"

"Take those blasted platters with you," Ellen cawed from the bottom of the ladder. After whacking the ceiling with her broom handle, she grumbled downstairs for a cup of tea.

After You've Gone descended from the rafters, This was Mr. Beasley's signature song.

★ ★ ★

Ellen awoke in her reading chair and stared blankly at the clock on the mantelpiece. She stood up, stretched, and listened: the house was still and chilled. *Is it really two in the morning?* Beasley was not in bed. He was probably asleep in the attic, leaving the skylight open again.

"Beasley?" Silence. "Raymond Eliot Beasley, come down to bed—immediately!" The loft ladder was still in place. *Better go up and find him.*

★ ★ ★

When the Beasleys' son Alan and his wife Kathy arrived for breakfast, they found the house unlocked, with Ellen asleep in the empty attic. "Mum, it's *freezing* up here," Alan cried, moving his mother towards the ladder. "Why did you leave the skylight open?"

"Come down, now," Kathy said. "We want to talk to you about Ferncroft."

"It's great, Mum," Alan said.

"They'll have a lovely room ready in February," Kathy added.

"But the attic?" Ellen said. "And Beasley's stuff—what about all that junk?"

"It's empty now," Alan said.

"Left, didn't he?" Ellen paused, hands on hips staring at the roof. "Went right through that skylight, the old mule!" She smiled. "Told me he would."

Dr. Hodgkins Goes to Heaven

It was nearly dawn. Fifty-two-year-old Christopher Hodgkins—Ph.D., world-renowned author, philosopher, and religious scoffer—was exhausted from yet another round of literary parties celebrating his latest book, an exposé ridiculing American hypocrisy, religious righteousness, corporate-funded televangelists, and corrupt right-wing talk-show hosts.

When his Aston Martin took flight off California Highway over Big Sur, Hodgkins witnessed scenes from his future unspool before him in slow motion, like a film. In his will, Christopher Hodgkins had stipulated that no services or clergy be allowed within a mile of his final resting place. However, as Hodgkins and his automobile were soon to be lost at sea, presumably forever, the question of a proper service would be moot.

From George Washington to Ronald Reagan: God Rules the White House soon became his most controversial bestseller. Pompous, irreverent, and unapologetic, some felt this book had gone too far, and that it was only a matter of time before something horrible happened to Dr. Hodgkins.

While preparing for icy salt water to seep into his car amidst a rush of hungry fish, Hodgkins felt his body gently dragged out of the drink, then borne skyward towards a silent void. Glancing back over his shoulder, he was appalled, watching his luxurious new vehicle sink into oblivion.

"I don't know what the devil's going on here," Hodgkins shouted while struggling to stay calm, "but if it's a joke, I damn well want it to stop."

Silence.

He tried a softer tone. "Look here. I'm tired and want to get home to bed." His voice vanished into a whisper. "This is not reasonable. I want answers now. Where the hell am I going?"

No response.

Dr. Hodgkins ascended silently towards a pulsating glow of vast celestial bodies. "What in Heaven's name could that be? The Aurora Borealis?" he grumbled.

His body continued to rise, growing lighter by the moment. Suddenly, a peculiar prickly sensation enveloped his entire being. He felt well! Despite his recent plunge into the sea, he was neither wet nor bloody nor suffering from any injuries. His hands, arms, and legs had become transparent—he could see *through* himself as if his entire body had been transformed from flesh, blood, and bones into a translucent morph.

This damn well had better be a dream.

★ ★ ★

Renowned atheist and notorious alcoholic Christopher Worthington Hodgkins was an arrogant and humorless man, parodied in cartoons as a crude country oaf—obese and disheveled, with hair plastered over a sweaty forehead and raised fists. However tactless and ill-mannered, Dr. Hodgkins possessed a vast intelligence and a quick wit that TV talk-show hosts found entertaining and a guaranteed rating booster. Whenever anyone publicly challenged his dogma, Christopher Hodgkins offered the same response: A snicker, a snort, and a sneer. The audience loved it.

Abruptly, his celestial journey ceased. Hodgkins landed upright and undamaged on level ground. He heard the hiss of wind but could feel no air. He found himself surrounded by iridescent, plant-like objects resembling bushes while dwarfed trees grew from a cork-like substance upon which he stood. *He had to be dreaming.*

Beyond these green growths, he could see gleaming patches of blue and golden fog hovering over an alien landscape; he could smell an aroma reminiscent of incense. Hodgkins loathed incense and waved his hands frantically, trying to clear the air, except there seemed to be no air anywhere despite the fact that he had no difficulty breathing.

"For God's sake, where the hell am I?" he shouted.

"Hell has nothing to do with it!" thundered a low voice, rumbling like rolling bowling balls directly over his head. Startled, Hodgkins looked upwards, downwards, then behind him, but nobody was visible.

Shaken by this ungodly sound, Dr. Hodgkins spoke more respectfully. "What's going on—is this some kind of joke?"

"Only if *you* think it to be so," rumbled the reply.

"Look, I just asked where—"

"And *I* told you, *hell* had nothing to do with it, didn't I?"

Hodgkins thought a moment. "So, I got drunk, and now I'm on the set of some lousy movie and—"

"Yes, go on." The ominous voice came closer.

"And I'm some hapless earthling, abducted and forced to live on an alien planet. Stupid story—it's been done a million times, hasn't it?"

For a moment, all was silent aside from the occasional rustling of plants and bushes. "You are not alone," rumbled the thunder.

"Look, whoever you are, why not show yourself and stop woofing into that megaphone or whatever you're using."

A twittering sound prompted Hodgkins to whirl about, confronted by a congregation of tall, slender, tree-like objects with smiling faces. Suddenly, searing flashes of bright orange and violet lightning forked the air, followed by a thunderclap.

"Look up, Christopher. Look *up!*" the voice commanded.

To Hodgkins's astonishment, a glowing column of churning lavender clouds appeared. Suddenly, a wraith emerged, enshrouded by long yellow hair, a complete, flowing beard, and huge hands with long, protruding fingers.

"Greetings, Christopher Hodgkins. Welcome to your new domain!" The specter floated in closer, eyes twinkling.

"My *domain?*" Dr. Hodgkins asked. "What in the hell are you talking about?"

"Dammit! Don't you *ever* listen? I told you, *hell* has nothing to do with it. Oh, by the way, Christopher, you'll be sharing this domain, or *neighborhood*, with everyone else, including me." The phantom's thunderous voice turned into waterfalls of laughter.

"All right, I'll bite," Hodgkins replied. "Who *are* you?"

The wraith coasted leisurely to the ground. For a moment, all was silent. "Can't you guess?"

"Look, I don't know who put you up to this, but I'm exhausted so, if you don't mind, let's get on with it . . . I want some sleep."

"Christopher—may I call you by your, uh, *Christian* name?"

"Yes, yes! Whatever."

The wraith forced a ghastly grin. "Christopher, old chap, since you don't want to believe that I exist, I'll simply offer you my nickname, OK?"

"What is it, then, for Christ's sake?" Hodgkins yawned.

"For now, you may refer to me as . . . The Big G, or Big G, for short. How's that?"

"Jolly good, Big G! Sounds great."

There was no reply.

"Christopher, you look like you could use some sleep." Big G's tone grew softer.

"I'm exhausted," Hodgkins yawned.

"All right then. I have some appointments to keep. One of the Dribbles will show you to your quarters."

Curiosity emboldened Dr. Hodgkins. "What sort of appointments, and what the devil are *Dribbles?*"

"This afternoon, I'm interviewing a whole group of new arrivals. Later, I promised Spinoza a game of chess. We play quite regularly."

"Spinoza? You don't mean the great Enlightenment philosopher, do you? You mean some guy you named Spinoza, right?"

"Baruch and I have debated for centuries."

"Why, of course, you have," Hodgkins replied, figuring he'd better humor this eccentric old bluffer.

"You'll meet him yourself, should you decide to stay. I'm certain it would be an uplifting conversation." Big G's chuckle came as a low roll of thunder. "Now, Dr. Hodgkins, meet the Dribbles—just behind you."

A rising bank of clouds enveloped Big G as Hodgkins whirled about to see a pair of grinning tree-like creatures standing only a foot away, one short and one tall, holding out their branching arms in signs of welcome and peace.

"We'll show you to your quarters, now, Christopher," said the taller Dribble in a dreamy tone that sounded far away. "You need some rest."

"I hope you won't think I'm impertinent for the asking," Hodgkins replied, "but why are you all so *green*?"

"It's the latest thing, isn't it?" said the shorter Dribble in a high-pitched and wobbly tone. "It's because we are an entirely herbivorous species around here—no meat, no fish, no fowl."

"Sounds disgustingly wholesome and healthy."

"Yes, and no *alcohol* or *cigarettes*," the tall Dribble said, shaking its finger at Hodgkins as both Dribbles broke into laughter.

"Wholly organic, you see," squealed the smaller Dribble, bouncing up and down with glee. "We mean green, green, green—that's the scene."

"And say, have you heard that green is the most restful color for the eyes?" the tall Dribble asked, winking at Hodgkins.

"I am *not* amused!" Hodgkins cried, irritated by their attempts to mock him. "Now, I'd like to get back home as quickly as possible, if you don't mind."

"In due course," the tall Dribble replied, "But now, it's time for you to sleep."

Directing Hodgkins to turn about, the Dribbles pointed towards an odd, columnar hut that resembled a small igloo dipped in chlorophyll. As they led him to his quarters, Hodgkins looked beyond the cottage. He noticed this new domain stretched out further than the eye could see—an infinite, shimmering plane of celestial matter, light and dark, possessing neither a top nor a bottom nor, it appeared, limits of any kind.

A damn good job of glass painting. Hodgkins now believed he had been cast into someone's fantasy film.

The Dribbles led Hodgkins to an opening into the green hut and bade him farewell.

The hut appeared to have no conventional doors or windows, only gaps. Inside were two dimly lit cubicles. One contained what seemed to be a bed and a chair cloaked in plain gray cloth. The other appeared to be a small eating area, but the walls had built-in bookshelves displaying great philosophers' and essayists' works, all with green leather bindings.

"Looks like the Harvard Classics made it to Heaven." Hodgkins wondered why he had thought that, but since he was not on Earth at all and because God did not exist, this could *not* be Heaven, could it? Hodgkins didn't know what to think, but now he was exhausted.

He flopped down on what felt like the most comfortable bed he had ever known. Soon darkness enveloped the room, and he succumbed to a deep sleep filled with nightmares about his first book, *God Is a Fraud—Religion Is a Racket*. The book's premise was simple: "God is a myth, religion is rubbish, ecclesiastics are charlatans, and their followers nothing better than witless sheep. It's all about money and manipulation, always has been." Though the bestseller had earned him distinction at home and abroad, he was blackballed from the Church of England and publicly criticized by the Archbishop of Canterbury. Ayatollahs had issued multiple fatwas against him, and he had received truckloads of hate mail from right-wing religious leaders in the U.S. As more controversy meant more sales, all of this was to his delight. After all, luxury sports cars and premium hooch were not cheap.

But in his dream, the book was causing worldwide chaos. His words had infuriated millions, throwing religious institutions and governments into conflict, triggering strikes, and fomenting violent street demonstrations in hundreds of cities.

Scenes from the nightmare grew intense and confusing, overlapping without any logic. Suddenly, Hodgkins saw himself back in America, where his book was banned. God was getting good press as churches, synagogues, and mosques were filled to overflowing in a world gone mad. Politicians and clerics across America went rabid. Senators from evangelical states demanded a national surtax to cover the cost of pursuing and capturing Christopher Hodgkins. At the same time, conservative clerics cried for increased collections in all organized religions because they said God was under attack.

God had ascended again, and churches, synagogues, and mosques were packed. A Texas congressman proposed a statute requiring mandatory Bible study in every school. Legislators began probing all public officials' birthplace and baptismal records in Louisiana and Alabama, including the sitting President.

TV networks, battling for interviews and revenues, rewarded talk-show hosts who demanded that Hodgkins be tarred and feathered, boiled in oil, or hung—preferably a combination of all three. Dr. Hodgkins was now an outcast, a heathen, an illegal alien. Only New Hampshire abstained from the fray, offering Hodgkins sanctuary. Conservatives swiftly condemned this small state in New England as "a godless state that ought to secede from the union."

But what else could he have done? Sit back and let those nitwit dominionists in government carry on? Keep silent while yet another American president declared war, citing divine direction? Had not enough blood been shed in the name of God and country?

Hodgkins found himself cowering in his own home, peering through his living room window as hordes of maniacal clergy, backed by religious extremists carrying crucifixes, picketed his home and neighborhood, holding placards that said, "Burn Hodgkins," "Lynch Hodgkins," and "Send Hodgkins to Hell." A rock smashed through his window, bashing his forehead. Torches were lit, burning crosses rose, and white hoods were donned as the crazed crowds shoved their way like human wedges up the pathway to his front door, their eyes glowing as they chanted in a hollow monotone, "Get him, get him, get him!" As the shouting grew louder, a barrage of bricks crashed through his living room window, and a flaming torch landed on the carpet.

"No!" Hodgkins yelled, waking up and lurching forward in bed, drenched in sweat. "I won't recant!" He sat upright, trembling, close to tears.

A voice in the darkened room startled him. "Having a bad dream, are we, Christopher?" Big G was standing at the end of his bed, *glowing like a bloody plastic dashboard-Jesus*, thought Hodgkins.

Hodgkins rubbed his eyes as he stared at the electrically charged phantom. "I have woken from one nightmare, only to find myself locked in another."

He trembled as he struggled to stand. His throat was parched. "I could use a libation right about now," he said.

"In your kitchenette, you'll find a nice variety of sparkling and natural waters. Oh, and by the way, Christopher, we have no use for alcohol here."

"Here?" Dr. Hodgkins asked. "Now tell me, please, *where* are we, anyway?"

Big G chuckled. "Guess."

Another trap. Hodgkins thought momentarily and then

decided to change the subject by pointing towards the bookshelves. "I see you have my work here."

"Yes, of course. Our library would be incomplete if we didn't have *you* in the stacks, hey?" Big G paused to thoughtfully stroke his flowing beard. He then wandered over to one of the bookshelves, reached up, and pulled down a copy of *God is a Fraud*. Christopher Hodgkins had resigned himself to the situation: he was being held prisoner by some mad, celestial dictator calling himself 'Big G,' pretending to be 'God.' *I better play my cards with caution.*

Absorbed in his reading, Big G did not notice that a Dribble had entered the room until it spoke. "Sorry to disturb you, but Spinoza says it's time for chess."

"Baruch Spinoza? Time for chess?" Hodgkins was incredulous. "Prove it. I want to meet the man myself...right now."

"All in good time, Christopher," Big G chuckled, placing the book back onto a shelf.

"Why not *now*?" asked Hodgkins. *Typical arrogant despot.*

"Relax, Christopher. When we're ready. But first, we need to sort you out."

Hodgkins became livid. "Now, hang on a moment! Do I not have the liberty to think and speak as I choose?"

"You and everyone else have free will, always have." Big G drifted towards the doorway of the green igloo. "It's one of your finest assets." He turned to leave. "We shall talk again soon. Have a great day."

"Love your costume!" Hodgkins shouted at the fleeting specter. Needing a cold drink, he charged into the kitchenette. After gulping something that tasted like seltzer water and spitting it out, Hodgkins quickly left the room. He wandered towards the igloo doorway and found the tallest Dribble watching him with amusement.

"How about a tour of your domain?" the smallest creature asked. Hodgkins noticed a few more Dribbles standing outside the igloo, staring and grinning.

"Sure, why not?" Hodgkins followed and stood facing a group of grinning Dribbles. "Look here. Do you find something funny about me?"

"No, not you," they replied in unison.

"But your last book sure gave us a good giggle," snickered the younger Dribble. "Shall we?"

The older Dribble led the way, and in what seemed like only a moment, Hodgkins found himself standing at the base of a great mountain, rising into a multi-colored fog.

"Am I supposed to meet someone here?" Hodgkins asked.

"Soon. Let's take a ramble," the older Dribble said, taking Hodgkins's hand and leading him towards the walking path encircling the mountain. When Hodgkins looked back, he saw more Dribbles in a long line, following at a distance.

They had only climbed a short way up the mountain when an ethereal voice called out, startling Hodgkins and causing the Dribbles to twitter. "Hello, Hodgkins! Welcome to Orwell's Place!"

Hodgkins looked about frantically but could not see anyone. "Is that you, George?"

"Up here, chum," the voice bellowed. "Oh, sorry! Can't see me yet, can you?"

Hodgkins stared at the Dribbles, shrugging his shoulders. "What does he mean?"

The older Dribble pretended to look serious. "Well, you're not officially *here*, are you, Christopher? This is only a trial run, isn't it? You might call it *limbo*."

Hodgkins was confused. "I don't know *where* I am, so I can't possibly answer, can I?"

The Dribbles nodded in agreement. "He can't answer until he understands the question, can he?" they answered in unison.

The older Dribble began to chuckle. "We'll just have to ask Big G if—"

A muted thunderclap startled Hodgkins, forcing him to

whirl about. There appeared Big G, emerging out of the uppermost clouds. "I can answer your query," rumbled Big G, floating down from the upper plateau.

"Did you have a good game?" asked one of the Dribbles.

Big G smacked his hands together, producing another explosion that made Hodgkins jump.

"I wish you'd quit doing that," Hodgkins shouted. "It's very goddam annoying."

"Sorry, old man," Big G said, pretending to be contrite. "I get a bit carried away whenever I've been with Spinoza. Anyway, the old bugger tried to cheat during our game."

"Again?" the Dribbles cried, laughing so hard they could hardly stand.

"Again!" Big G roared. "He knows better or ought to, but what the hell—he gets a kick out of trying to outwit the Old Man, doesn't he?"

The Dribbles continued laughing and nodding, winking their bright green eyes at one another like Christmas tree lights gone berserk.

"Now, to our friend Christopher Hodgkins," said Big G. "He has a decision to make, doesn't he?"

"Whether or not to stay—right?" Hodgkins asked.

"Your choice, chum," Big G replied. "No hurry, you'll have time—all the time in the world."

★ ★ ★

Throughout this strange habitation and in the company of these peaceful green creatures—kind, humorous, and gentle—Hodgkins pondered a world he could never have imagined. His defenses and his petulance had slowly weakened over time.

With the Dribbles escorting Hodgkins, the walking group arrived near the summit of a mysterious mountain. Embedded deeply was the notion that time was without effort; it was either not passing or passing very quickly. Looking about, Hodgkins perceived he could feel pulsating presences all around him. The mountain, he knew intuitively, housed millions, perhaps billions, of spirits residing somewhere within—without form and heard only as occasional whispers—arriving and departing like shards of memory. Hodgkins felt curiously free and satisfied, almost cheerful for the first time since childhood.

High over his head, Hodgkins beheld a projected image that seemed to develop out of nothing, turning brighter and more transparent as he watched. He now recognized a favorite photograph from his mother's family album—of himself as a boy of six, his father holding him, his mother looking on. It was the last time he remembered being truly happy—not yet traumatized by scary church sermons on original sin, decrepit Sunday school teachers, or embittered clergy.

Tears began streaming down Hodgkin's face. "Hello, Mother?"

Silence.

The older Dribble took Hodgkins by the arm. "Time to go," he said. The Dribbles led Hodgkins to a vast, wide-open area that looked like grassland on Earth—lush and blossoming with flower-like objects that waved to an airless breeze. The entire panorama appeared dotted with the odd, green-hued igloos, similar to the one where he had slept the previous night.

"Can you see that little hut down below?" the older Dribble asked.

Searching the base of a gently sloping hillock, Hodgkins saw a miniature igloo, partially camouflaged by verdant groves of sultry plants that looked like elephants' ears.

"Yes," Hodgkins replied, "I can see it."

"Big G is waiting for you, Christopher," the tallest Dribble bubbled.

Now, Hodgkins stood alone, anxious about his forthcoming encounter with Big G and weary of this gassy, grassy environment filled with strange beings and elements utterly foreign to everything he had ever known. He missed his whiskey, pretty women, and fancy cars. He moreover wanted to return home to re-engage all those fools he battled with regularly on television. Reluctantly, Hodgkins began his walk towards the hut at the bottom of the slope.

Big G was waiting for him in the doorway.

"Ah, Christopher, good. Welcome to my humble abode." Big G beckoned him forward, and in a moment, Dr. Hodgkins found himself inside the hut, seated on what looked and felt like a soft rubber bench. He was surprised that everything looked remarkably like his own hut. "You look perplexed, my dear fellow," rumbled Big G.

"I suppose I expected something . . . different," Hodgkins replied.

"More exalted?"

"Yeah, you know—scepters and diadems. All that crap."

Big G laughed. "Your problem, chum, is that you have always taken everything so literally—and far too seriously."

Hodgkins lost his temper. "Now look, dammit, I didn't come here for a lecture."

"Why, then, did you come?"

Hodgkins rose and waggled his finger at Big G. "Not for you to 'sort me out.' Look here; it's all rubbish, anyway. Smoke and mirrors, myth, and myrrh. I'll have none of it; you don't exist, nor do Heaven or hell. We have enough practical evidence to prove scientifically—"

"Oh, for God's sake, shut up, will you?" Big G shouted, sounding like roaming bowling balls.

Hodgkins sat down; his face was red and sweaty.

"Look at you," Big G cried. "You behave precisely like those fire and brimstone fools back on Earth."

"Failure, Big G. Failure! Two hundred thousand years and still—"

"Yes, yes, yes. Now, Christopher, we have all read your books, listened to your bloody speeches, and suffered those interminable, humorless, one-sided debates. Still, *nobody*, not even *you*, can explain the order of things. Without a divine hand, where would humanity have developed? Out of Microbes? Cosmic dust? Come on, man, use your noodle."

"Why don't you just tell the truth?" Hodgkins mopped beads of sweat from his forehead.

"Listen for a moment, and look at things from my view," cried Big G. "Humanity has been endowed with the greatest of all gifts—free will—and how has the species responded? War, plunder, and rape, to say nothing of robbery, racism, despotism, torture, kidnapping, adultery, homicide, and genocide."

"You overlooked televangelism," Hodgkins interrupted.

Big G rolled his eyes. "Can't think of everything, can I?"

"Your great sublime vision has *failed*!" Hodgkins cried triumphantly.

Big G sighed. "I had a better order in mind; truly, I did."

"Besides," Hodgkins continued, "We all know that nobody *made* the universe—or galaxies if you prefer."

"Which universe, Christopher? I look after so many, you know."

"Well, the solar system planet Earth occupies, just to name one."

Big G stood and began to pace about the room. "What *is* your problem, Christopher? You've had a good life. So, where's the gratitude?"

"Gratitude? Gratitude? Why the hell should we show *gratitude*, hey? Humanity has not exactly been a smashing success, has it? Two hundred thousand years, more or less, pounding this planet, and we're still subjected to the most horrendous suffering, horrible diseases, old-age disability, all capped off by an unpredictable and often painful death—"

"Are *you* lecturing *me*?"

"Great work you do," Hodgkins shouted. "We suffer drought, famine, floods, pestilence, plagues, horrendous earthquakes, volcanic eruption, catastrophic climatic change, and future cataclysmic collisions with other galaxies. Well done!"

"Don't overlook avalanches and asteroids," Big G roared back. "Perhaps you have a superior plan, Mr. Answer Man? Or shall we all sit back and take pity on this poor primate?"

Hodgkins threw up his hands in surrender. "Well, *someone* created this god-awful mess. Who the hell will clean it up?"

"Gotcha!" A hazy blur began to form around Big G. "It's the great ontological argument, isn't it?" Big G held out his long-fingered hands in a sign of farewell before evaporating into a rising mist.

"Wait!" Hodgkins called out. "I've decided—I want to go back. Yes, back home, now."

Big G evaporated, his voice barely audible. "Very well, Christopher, so it shall be." His voice drifted into cotton. "Free will, remember?"

★ ★ ★

Christopher Hodgkins was sound asleep in a recliner when the telephone began ringing. From the depths of his slumber, he detected something far away and tried to ignore it, but the ringing persisted. He knew it was *his* telephone, imperious and unrelenting.

It must be Kate, Hodgkins thought from his subconscious midst.

He picked up the phone and mumbled, "Is it you, Kate?"

"Are you all right?" It was Kate's all-too-familiar, lawyerly interrogation. "I've been calling for two days. What's going on, Chris?"

"I've been drunk for at least that duration and possibly longer," he replied.

"Chris, Dr. Wang phoned me last week with your test results. He's concerned that you never return his calls."

"Yes? And?"

"And you need to go see Dr. Philobosian about your heart—"

"My *heart*?" Hodgkins laughed. "I thought he'd have something terrifying to say about my *liver*. My heart's in the highlands, and it's just fine, thanks very much."

"Seems you've got CHD—you'll need to go on medication."

"CHD? Right now, Kate, all I have is a headache from listening to your bloody babble."

For a moment, neither spoke.

"How's your new car?" Kate asked.

"Drove it straight into the ocean a few days ago."

"Of course you did," Kate said, her tone softening. "With you in it, naturally."

"That's right," he said. "Anyway, I'm back home safe and sound." He paused again. "You OK, Kate?"

"Yes, fine. It's Halloween, so I must run and get candy at the store."

"Halloween? I forgot all about it."

"Better go get something for the kids."

"Free candy for kids—nasty little truants are threatening tricks every year. What a goddam racket."

"OK, Chris, gotta go," Kate replied. "Don't forget Dr. Philobosian."

"I will," he replied.

"You will *what*?"

"I *will* forget about Dr. Philobosian. There's another swindle—heart surgeons, all those overpriced, over-rated *specialists*. They and Big Pharma will bleed you dry. Look, when you go, you go, that's it. Lights out. Why prolong the stay?"

There was another brief silence. "Take care of yourself, Christopher, and don't forget to bring the kids some candy." She hung up.

Hodgkins sat back down in his chair, annoyed; Kate had called and woken him with her nasty medical stuff. When the doorbell rang, he was just about to sit back and reflect on his most recent and fantastic hallucination about a meeting with some green creatures and a celestial dictator calling himself Big G. He looked at his watch and noticed it was almost

Dr. Hodgkins Goes to Heaven

six-thirty. As he rose from his chair and went to open the door, Dr. Hodgkins felt a quick, sharp pain piercing his chest like an ice pick. *I'll have to explain to these trick-or-treating little beggars that I'm not feeling well.* He took a deep breath and swung the door open.

What he saw astounded him; his heart and breathing stopped for a second. Waiting at the door were two tall, smiling green creatures, arms outstretched, enveloped in a light mist, and smelling like a strangely familiar perfume—perhaps incense. Hodgkins's first impulse was to crack a joke: *Where did you get those fantastic costumes?* But another stabbing pain stopped him short. Dizzy, and now filled with dread, he sank to his knees, gripping his chest.

Fragments of his life passed through a dimming consciousness as Hodgkins struggled to breathe; scenes of Christmas at home and birthday parties when he was a little boy; commencement from university; his first journey to America, and the marriage to Kate; his first book...

When the twin Dribbles stepped forward to assist him, Hodgkins held his hands out in supplication. "I'm not such a bad fellow, you know. I've just tried to—you know—get people to be sensible."

"You have a rendezvous with Spinoza, Christopher," replied one of the Dribbles, smiling while stepping forward to lift him from the floor.

The moment he found himself enfolded within the Dribbles' loving arms Hodgkin's distress began to fade. A beam brighter than daylight burst through the doorway, so intense that he had to close his eyes to its brilliance. In a scene from childhood, he heard faraway phrases of his favorite music— *Dream of Gerontius*—and noticed his entire body had turned crystalline.

As the beam of white light dimmed, he closed his eyes. While Gerontius sang, a wave of ineffable pleasure filled his spirit, releasing Christopher Hodgkins from a lifetime of loneliness and anger.

"At last," he thought, "I have found my Cockaigne."

About Atmosphere Press

Atmosphere Press is an independent, full-service publisher for excellent books in all genres and for all audiences. Learn more about what we do at atmospherepress.com.

We encourage you to check out some of Atmosphere's latest releases, which are available at Amazon.com and via order from your local bookstore:

Icarus Never Flew 'Round Here, by Matt Edwards

COMFREY, WYOMING: Maiden Voyage, by Daphne Birkmeyer

The Chimera Wolf, by P.A. Power

Umbilical, by Jane Kay

The Two-Blood Lion, by Nick Westfield

Shogun of the Heavens: The Fall of Immortals, by I.D.G. Curry

Hot Air Rising, by Matthew Taylor

30 Summers, by A.S. Randall

Delilah Recovered, by Amelia Estelle Dellos

A Prophecy in Ash, by Julie Zantopoulos

The Killer Half, by JB Blake

Ocean Lessons, by Karen Lethlean

Unrealized Fantasies, by Marilyn Whitehorse

The Mayari Chronicles: Initium, by Karen McClain

Squeeze Plays, by Jeffrey Marshall

JADA: Just Another Dead Animal, by James Morris

Hart Street and Main: Metamorphosis, by Tabitha Sprunger

Karma One, by Colleen Hollis

Ndalla's World, by Beth Franz

Adonai, by Arman Isayan

About the Author

Born in Concord, Massachusetts, **Nathaniel S. Johnson**, a veteran American radio broadcaster and sound engineer, is a Grammy-nominated record producer and the author of fiction and non-fiction.

An audio engineer, Mr. Johnson pioneered the implementation of Dolby Surround Sound® on compact discs for both the RCA Red Seal and RCA Victor labels.

The author of several novels, screenplays, and a collection of short stories, Mr. Johnson's most recent book, *Phoebe and Fred*, was published by Atmosphere Press. *One Before Bedtime* is Mr. Johnson's first published volume of short stories, appearing exclusively with Atmosphere.

Made in United States
North Haven, CT
09 September 2025